Dear Parents and Educators,

Welcome to Penguin Young Readers! As parents and educators, you know that each child develops at his or her own pace—in terms of speech, critical thinking, and, of course, reading. Penguin Young Readers recognizes this fact. As a result, each Penguin Young Readers book is assigned a traditional easy-to-read level (1–4) as well as a Guided Reading Level (A–P). Both of these systems will help you choose the right book for your child. Please refer to the back of each book for specific leveling information. Penguin Young Readers features esteemed authors and illustrators, stories about favorite characters, fascinating nonfiction, and more!

Bake, Mice, Bake!

LEVEL 1

GUIDED READING LEVEL **D**

This book is perfect for an **Emergent Reader** who:
- can read in a left-to-right and top-to-bottom progression;
- can recognize some beginning and ending letter sounds;
- can use picture clues to help tell the story; and
- can understand the basic plot and sequence of simple stories.

Here are some **activities** you can do during and after reading this book:
- Picture Clues: Use the pictures to tell the story. "Read" the illustrations. Can you tell from the mice's faces and movements what they might be thinking or saying to one another?
- Rhyming Words: On a separate sheet of paper, make a list of all the rhyming words in this story. For example, *cake* rhymes with *bake*, so write those two words next to each other.

Remember, sharing the love of reading with a child is the best gift you can give!

—Bonnie Bader, EdM
   Penguin Young Readers program

*Penguin Young Readers are leveled by independent reviewers applying the standards developed by Irene Fountas and Gay Su Pinnell in Matching Books to Readers: Using Leveled Books in Guided Reading, Heinemann, 1999.

To Katie Carella, many thanks!—ES

To my mum, my dad, and my brother:
three very busy mice—NR

Penguin Young Readers
Published by the Penguin Group
Penguin Group (USA) Inc., 375 Hudson Street, New York, New York 10014, USA
Penguin Group (Canada), 90 Eglinton Avenue East, Suite 700, Toronto, Ontario M4P 2Y3, Canada
(a division of Pearson Penguin Canada Inc.)
Penguin Books Ltd., 80 Strand, London WC2R 0RL, England
Penguin Group Ireland, 25 St. Stephen's Green, Dublin 2, Ireland (a division of Penguin Books Ltd.)
Penguin Group (Australia), 250 Camberwell Road, Camberwell, Victoria 3124, Australia
(a division of Pearson Australia Group Pty. Ltd.)
Penguin Books India Pvt. Ltd., 11 Community Centre, Panchsheel Park, New Delhi—110 017, India
Penguin Group (NZ), 67 Apollo Drive, Rosedale, Auckland 0632, New Zealand
(a division of Pearson New Zealand Ltd.)
Penguin Books (South Africa) (Pty.) Ltd., 24 Sturdee Avenue,
Rosebank, Johannesburg 2196, South Africa

Penguin Books Ltd., Registered Offices: 80 Strand, London WC2R 0RL, England

Library of Congress Control Number: 2011010817

ISBN 978-0-448-45763-5   10

BAKE, MICE, BAKE!

by Eric Seltzer

illustrated by Natascha Rosenberg

Penguin Young Readers
An Imprint of Penguin Group (USA) Inc.

Wake, mice, wake!

Run out the door.

Time to bake

at Cakes and More.

Mice crack and whip.

Mice pour and drip.

Mice cut and chop.

Mice drop and mop.

9

Mice stir and shake.

Mice smooth and bake.

Mice bake a cake.

Mice love to bake.

12

Dog comes.

Frog comes.

Moose comes.

Goose comes.

We need more cake.

So bake, mice, bake!

Cat comes.

Rat comes.

Snail comes.

Whale comes.

We need more cake.

So bake, mice, bake!

One cake for Bee.

Oh, make that three.

Fly comes by.

He wants pie.

The last cake goes.

The shop must close.

Put everything away.

We are done for the day.

Cherry tarts, berry tarts.

All the tarts are now in carts.

Clean up the shop.

Wipe up the floor.

Scrub and mop

at Cakes and More.

Mice can rest their feet.

Look!

One pie to eat.

Finish pie.

Wave good-bye.

31901063040622